HOW NOW BROWN COW

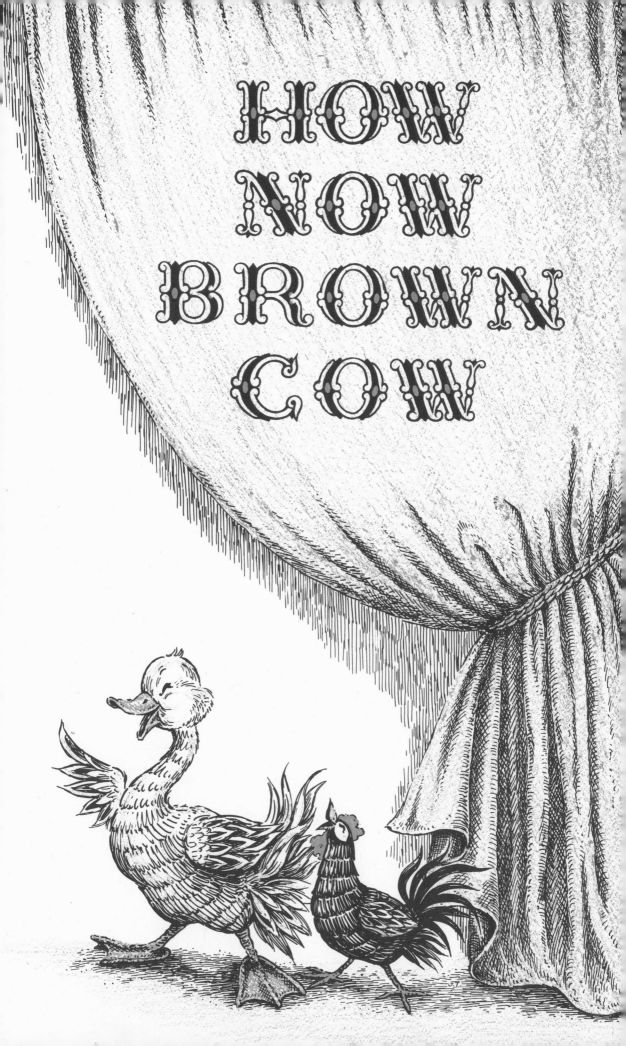

HOW NOW BROWN COW

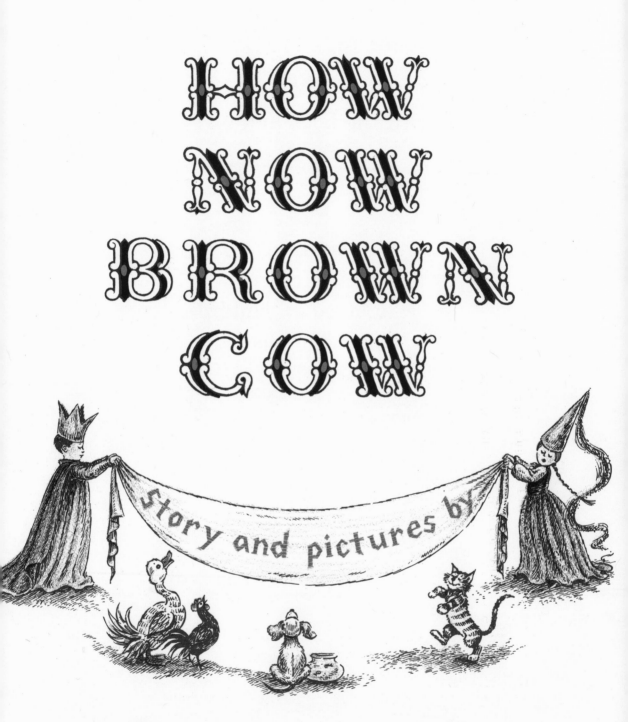

story and pictures by

Jean Tamburine

ABINGDON PRESS

Nashville   **New York**

To
All the boys and girls
everywhere

and for
Nell McVeigh
who loved all children
and who shared
this with me

"And I Wanted to Be the Princess..."

1

The duck, the hen, and the cat ran to the gate, but Susy took no notice of them. The school bus had brought Susy home. Her eyes were red from crying. Tears were shining on her cheeks, and her nose made sniffing noises as she ran.

"It's just not fair, Mother!" shouted Susy. "It was all my idea. I DON'T WANT TO BE THE LITTLE BROWN COW!"

"Wait a minute, Susy," said her mother. "Who wants you to be the little brown cow?"

"Miss Clancy!" Susy yelled.

"Miss Clancy? Your teacher?"

Now Susy was really crying. Great ugly sounds came from her throat and tears streamed from her eyes.

"I wanted to be the princess with the long golden curls, and she said—Miss Clancy said I had to be the little brown cow."

"Really, Susy," said Mother, "I don't understand. You just aren't making sense."

7

"What's wrong with her?" asked Susy's brother Bob, who had come home from school.

"Don't call me HER," Susy sobbed. "You know my name is Susy. I don't want to be the little brown cow. I want to be the princess with the long golden curls."

"Yeow!" whistled Bob. "I'd much rather be a cow than a princess. Do you have to be one or the other?"

"Miss Clancy said I couldn't be in the play unless I was the little brown cow, and I want to be the princess," sobbed Susy.

"You said that already," laughed Bob.

"Mother! Make him stop LOOKING at me!" Susy cried.

Bob shut his eyes very tight and said, "Would you move so I can reach the peanut butter? I would not want to step on your long golden curls—"

"MOTHER! Make him stop," screamed Susy.

"Both of you be quiet," Mother said. "Susy, can you tell me what this is all about?"

"We wrote stories at school today," Susy began. "Miss Clancy said we would act out the best story. She said if it was good enough we could have it in the auditorium and invite parents and everybody."

"Boy, that will be something," interrupted Bob. "LADIES AND GENTLEMEN, step right up. In this corner we have Susy, the little brown cow—"

"Oh, Bob, you think you are so smart," sniffled Susy. "I bet you couldn't write the best play."

"What did you write?" teased Bob. "Once upon a time there was the end?"

"You—you HORRIBLE PICKLE!" shouted Susy.

10

"Did you write the best story, Susy?" Mother asked. "How do you know it was best?"

"Yes, I did," sobbed Susy. "The boys and girls voted on the best story and mine won. Miss Clancy told us which parts to act out. And I'm just not going to be the little brown cow!"

"Susy," said her mother, "since you cannot stop crying, I think the only thing to do is call Miss Clancy."

"Don't call her," begged Susy. "She doesn't know how it feels to be an old brown cow."

"You feed your pets, Susy," Mother said. "I will decide about calling Miss Clancy."

2

Susy sat in her favorite place under the chinaberry tree and cried some more. The duck and the hen and the cat just stood and looked at her.

"Quack!" said the duck.

"Cluck! Cluck!" said the hen.

"Meow, meow, meow!" said the cat.

"Don't you laugh," cried Susy. "Something terrible has happened. Miss Clancy says I have to be an old brown cow—"

And the crying started all over again.

"Susy!" called Mother. "Your father is home and supper is ready. Wash your face and hands."

When they were all seated at the table, and Bob had said the blessing, Susy sat and stared at her plate. She studied the bubbles in her milk. She took deep, deep breaths, but she couldn't look at Mother and Father and Bob.

"Susy has a problem," Mother said to Father. "I talked with Miss Clancy a few minutes ago."

Susy's eyes grew round, and without thinking she looked straight at her father.

Mother went on: "Miss Clancy said that in school today all the boys and girls wrote stories. Then they voted to see which story they liked best, and they selected Susy's story. They are going to act it out in the auditorium. All of us are invited."

"That's very good, Susy," said Father.

Susy was looking at her plate and sliding down in her chair.

"Miss Clancy told the children which part each child would act out," Mother continued.

"AND I DON'T WANT TO BE THE LITTLE BROWN COW!" Susy shouted.

"Don't interrupt me, Susy," said Mother. "Miss Clancy told me that since Lisa's story had been chosen second best, she felt Lisa should be the princess. And Stevie, whose story was third best, should be the prince."

Susy looked up and added quickly, "And she said Dickie could be the jack-in-the-box. Rosa could be the mean old witch, and Theodore could be the clown. She went on and on giving parts to everybody. And finally," Susy sobbed, "she said I could be the little brown cow. It's not fair. The whole thing was MY IDEA."

"Susy," asked her father, "what did Lisa say when your story was chosen?"

"Not anything. She voted for my story."

"How about Stevie? What did he do?"

"He didn't do anything either, but he gets to be the prince. It was MY IDEA!"

"What good is an idea if you cannot make use of it?" asked Father.

"I don't know what you mean."

"Suppose nobody had wanted to be in your play?" asked Father. "First of all, suppose Miss Clancy had not given permission for the children to act out the story. What good would your idea have been then?"

Susy slid down in her chair so far she could hardly see the table.

"Miss Clancy told me something else," Mother said softly.

Susy closed her eyes and tried not to breathe.

"Miss Clancy said," continued Mother, "that when she told Susy she was to be the little brown cow, Susy stamped her foot and shouted 'I DON'T WANT TO BE THE LITTLE BROWN COW!'"

Father looked at Mother. "I wonder," said Father, "what the other boys and girls think of Susy."

"I can tell you," said Bob. "They think she is a poor sport. They think—"

"What's a poor sport?" Susy whispered.

"It is somebody who has to have his own way about everything. It is somebody who won't do anything for the team," said Father.

"I'm not on any team." Susy was louder now. "I'm just in the second grade. There isn't any team."

"Oh, yes, there is," said Father. "The whole second grade is a team, and you must do whatever is best for the whole team."

"Susy," said Mother. "You must apologize to Miss Clancy."

"What's a-pol-o-gize?"

"When you apologize, you tell someone you are sorry for something you have said or done and you ask him to forgive you."

"Could I whisper in Miss Clancy's ear?" asked Susy.

"Did you whisper when you told her you didn't want to be the little brown cow?"

Susy shook her head. "No," she said, looking down at her plate, "I sort of yelled. Must I yell when I apologize?"

"Miss Clancy would not like it if you yelled," said Mother, "but you must apologize in front of the whole class."

3

The next day, when all the boys and girls were listening, Susy said, "Miss Clancy, may I talk, please, Miss Clancy?"

"All right, Susy," said Miss Clancy.

"I'm sorry," Susy began. She stopped and then started again. "I'm sorry I didn't want to be the little brown cow. I wanted to be the princess." Susy looked around at the boys and girls. All of them were watching her.

"Thank you," said Susy, "for choosing my story."

"We accept your apology, Susy," Miss Clancy said. "And now I have something to ask you. Who should play the part of the little brown cow when we act out your story?"

Susy looked down at the floor. Then she looked up and said, "I will be the little brown cow."

And so every day the boys and girls worked very hard doing their arithmetic and geography and grammar. They rehearsed the play, and they made decorations and costumes. With cardboard and poster paint they made the school stage into a castle and courtyard. They made scenery and costumes from paper bags, cardboard, and grown-up clothes.

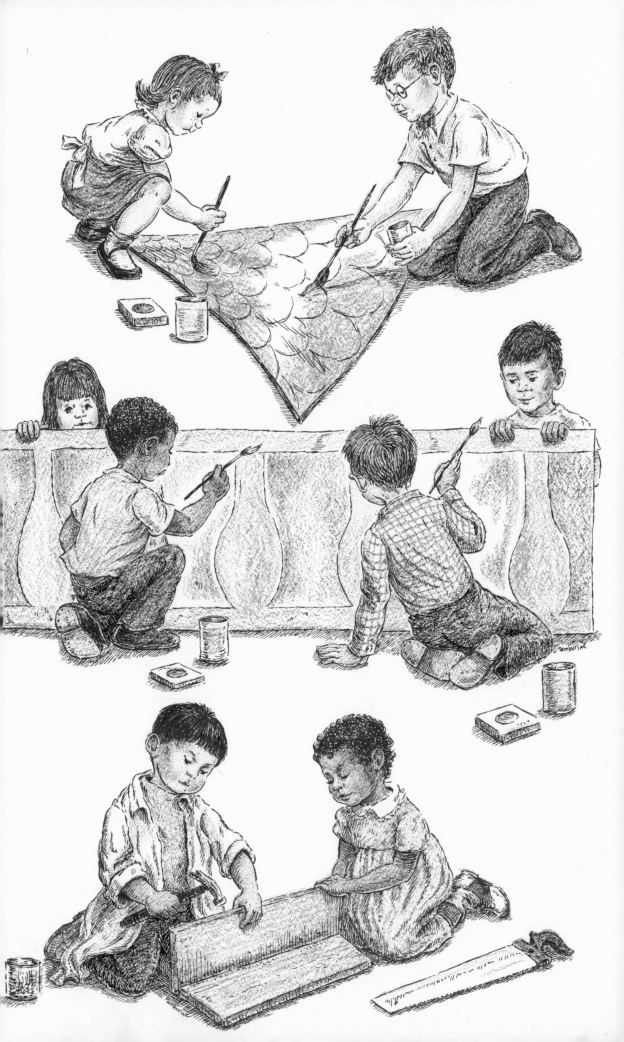

Soon it was the day to put on the play. Every seat in the auditorium was taken. Inuk, who was the very best reader in the second grade, stood at one side of the stage and read Susy's story in a loud, clear voice.

This is the story Inuk read:

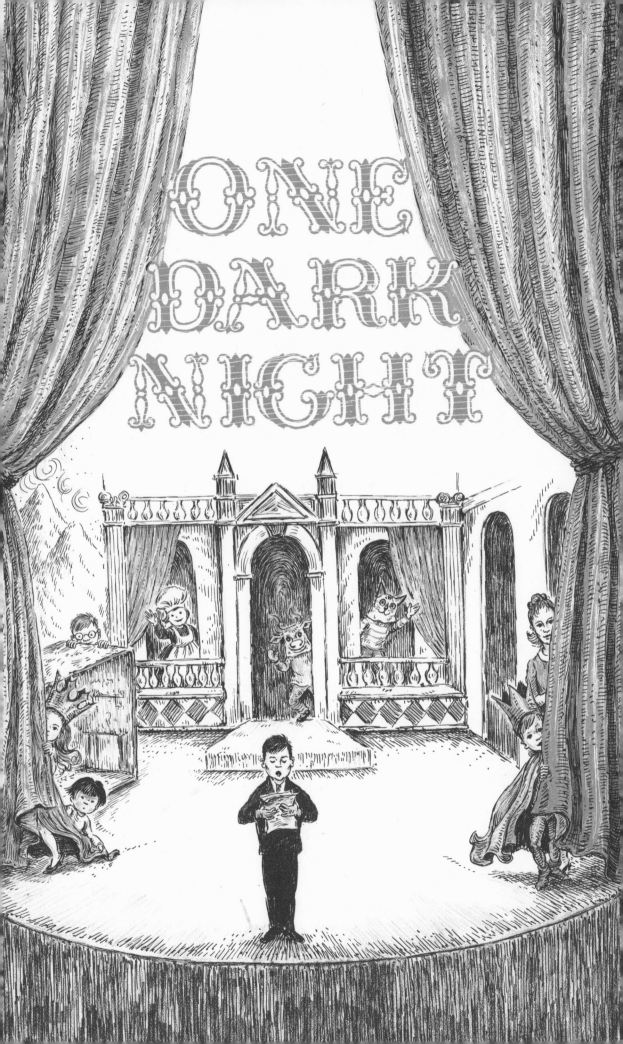

Once long ago in a big castle lived a king and a queen and a beautiful princess. It was a happy castle. Cheerful Cat lived in the castle. He belonged to the princess. He purred like music, so that everyone felt happy and good. That is why he was called Cheerful Cat.

(The king and queen and princess came onstage, followed by Cheerful Cat. As Inuk continued to read the story, other characters came onstage to act out what Inuk was reading.)

The people in the castle were nice to each other. The animals were treated nicely. The gardens grew more than enough food. There was only one person who was not happy. She was Mean Old Witch. She didn't like to see anyone be happy.

ONE DARK NIGHT
written by Susy, and
directed by Miss Clancy
acted by the whole
second grade class.

(Mean Old Witch stalked on stage, clawing the air with her hands. Behind her came Warty Toad. Mean Old Witch and Warty Toad stood at one side of the stage, apart from the king, queen, princess, and Cheerful Cat. Slowly the king, queen, princess, and Cheerful Cat moved off the stage.)

One dark night Mean Old Witch and her helper, Warty Toad, set out for the castle.

Mean Old Witch cackled, "I will spoil EVERYTHING in that happy castle. Hee! Hee! Hee!"

So Mean Old Witch and Warty Toad flew on her broomstick to the tower where Cheerful Cat slept near the princess.

(Mean Old Witch and Warty Toad straddled a broomstick and ran around the stage very fast. By this time the princess had come back on stage and was fast asleep at one side of the stage, with Cheerful Cat sleeping nearby.)

Quietly Mean Old Witch picked up
Cheerful Cat and put him inside her cloak.
Mean Old Witch and Warty Toad jumped
onto the broomstick and flew far away to
Black Mountain.

(The stage was darkened for a moment, and Cheerful
Cat ran offstage. He was replaced by three ladies-in-
waiting who stood near the princess when the lights
came on again. Inuk continued reading the story.)

The next morning the princess awoke. Cheerful Cat was nowhere to be seen.

"Where is my Cheerful Cat?" cried the princess.

"He is gone!" replied the ladies-in-waiting.

"Search for him!" cried the princess.

(While Inuk continued reading, all the boys and girls playing these parts pretended to look EVERYWHERE for Cheerful Cat.)

Everyone searched the castle. The king and queen searched. The ladies-in-waiting searched. The clown searched. The knights-in-armor searched. The cook searched.

1435680

Nobody could find Cheerful Cat.
The princess cried so much she became
sick. Everyone and everything was gloomy
at the castle.

"Call the doctor!" shouted the king.

(The doctor marched onstage carrying a doctor's
black case. He felt the princess' wrist.)

"She is very sick," said the doctor, "because she is unhappy. Keep her warm, and try to find Cheerful Cat IMMEDIATELY."

Everyone tried to make the princess feel better. The clown hopped and skipped about. He made funny faces and tried on silly hats. The princess did not smile.

(The clown had been onstage, performing for the
princess, and now two ladies-in-waiting came onstage,
pretending to carry a large jack-in-the-box. The
brightly painted box, which the ladies-in-waiting
pushed across the stage, had no bottom. Inside the
box a boy crouched and crept across the stage until he
was beside the princess. Then he jumped up and
shouted.)

"BOO TO YOU!"

Even the jack-in-the-box could not
make the princess smile.
The castle and everyone in it was so
unhappy.

Mean Old Witch had spoiled their happiness by stealing Cheerful Cat.

Who knew where Cheerful Cat had gone?

Someone knew.

Down the steep hill from the castle, and through the village and across the field, Little Brown Cow knew. She had heard Cheerful Cat scream as Mean Old Witch flew overhead.

"Help me, help me, Little Brown Cow!" screeched Cheerful Cat. "Mean Old Witch has got me!"

That was all Little Brown Cow heard, but she knew it was her friend Cheerful Cat. Little Brown Cow mooed to some fireflies nearby to follow Mean Old Witch to see where she took Cheerful Cat.

(The stage and auditorium were dark. Many fireflies—boys and girls with little flashlights—stood on stage, outside a castle window. As Inuk continued to read, the boys and girls blinked the flashlights on and off.)

Meanwhile the queen was reading to the princess, hoping she would fall asleep. Hundreds of fireflies appeared at the window of the room. Their light was so bright it was dazzling.

"Oh, Mother!" cried the princess.
"I have never seen so many fireflies."

"I've noticed the fireflies, too," said the queen. "They fly away and then come back, again and again."

"They want us to go with them," cried the princess.

"How do you know?" asked the queen.

"I know just the way I know things about Cheerful Cat and about all the other animals," answered the princess.

"The light of the fireflies reaches across the dark night like a chain of tiny stars," said the queen.

"They seem to lead toward Black Mountain," said the princess. "Do you suppose they know where Cheerful Cat is?"

As the princess said this, all the fireflies danced up and down so their lights looked as if they were nodding YES.

"They do know where Cheerful Cat is!" exclaimed the princess. "We must hurry!"

(The princess and the queen hurried offstage. The stage
was dark now. The princess and queen reappeared with
the king and the knights-in-armor. One small light
played on these characters, while on the still-dark part
of the stage the boys and girls who were playing the
parts of the fireflies blinked their flashlights off and on
as if to lead the princess and her followers.)

The princess, followed by the king
and queen and all the knights-in-armor,
walked into the dark night. Soon they
were surrounded by the bright lights of
the fireflies. They followed the fireflies
down the steep hill from the castle. At the
bottom of the hill, a duck who was a
friend of Cheerful Cat waddled up to the
princess.

44

"Quack!" said the duck. "I will help you find Cheerful Cat."

They followed the lights of the fireflies through the sleeping village. Outside the village gate they met a hen who also was a friend of Cheerful Cat.

"Cluck, cluck," said the hen. "I will help you find Cheerful Cat."

(The boy and girl playing the part of the duck and the hen had come onstage as Inuk read about them. Now, the princess, the king, and the queen, along with the duck and the hen, walked around the stage as the fireflies blinked their flashlights off and on. Inuk continued reading the story.)

They followed the lights of fireflies across
the fields. The fireflies made a ring of light

46

all around Little Brown Cow, who was standing in the field.

(Little Brown Cow had come onstage in the darkness. She had brought a cardboard fence, and she stood peering over the fence as the fireflies, blinking their lights on and off, formed a ring around her.)

"MOO! MOO! MOO!" cried Little Brown Cow to the princess. "I sent my friends the fireflies to get you. I heard Cheerful Cat cry out from Mean Old Witch's broom. She has made him a prisoner on Black Mountain. I will take you there."

(The stage was dark except for the flashlights of the
fireflies, leading Little Brown Cow and all the others,
who were walking round and round, pretending to go
to Black Mountain. Inuk read on.)

Soon they came to Black Mountain.
Little Brown Cow led the way because
she was such a good climber. Up, up they
climbed to the top of the mountain—Little
Brown Cow, the duck, the hen, the knights-
in-armor, the king, the queen, and the
princess.

Quietly, quietly they crept to the opening of the cave where Mean Old Witch and Warty Toad were so busy being bad they didn't see or hear them.

(Other boys and girls had carried on the darkened stage two huge cardboard cartons, painted to look like rock. The cartons had one wide opening so the audience could see the inside. Red and yellow tissue paper and a lighted flashlight were used for the make-believe fire under a big black kettle in the cave.)

They peered into the cave. Mean Old Witch was stirring some magic potion in a big black kettle. Warty Toad just sat watching her. Cheerful Cat was all tied up with string so he looked exactly like a spool of thread.

And lying there beside Cheerful Cat was a prince from a distant castle. The witch had put an evil spell on the prince, who was asleep.

Mean Old Witch looked up when

Little Brown Cow and all the others
stepped into the cave.

"Go away! Go away! All of you!
You will ruin my spell," screamed Mean
Old Witch.

51

"That prince has been asleep for three weeks! Don't you dare wake him up. And don't you dare go near Cheerful Cat or I will turn you all to stone!"

Little Brown Cow started toward Cheerful Cat. Mean Old Witch's eyes turned red with rage. She was furious because Little Brown Cow did not seem to be afraid of her. Mean Old Witch shrieked horrible, angry sounds. She clawed the air with her bony, knifelike hands as she advanced toward poor Little Brown Cow.

"Don't you DARE go near Cheerful Cat!" screamed the witch. "And that princess had better not KISS that prince. I'll tear you to pieces."

Little Brown Cow really wanted to run from the horrible witch, but she knew that she must help her friends. She lowered her head and pawed the ground. She charged at Mean Old Witch and butted so hard with her sharp horns that the witch did a somersault backward—right over her steaming black kettle.

(Little Brown Cow pretended to butt Mean Old Witch, who rolled over backward, shrieking and screaming as she rolled.)

The princess ran to the sleeping prince and kissed him. She broke the witch's spell and the prince awoke at once.

Mean Old Witch grabbed her broom, and Warty Toad jumped on the broomstick with her.

Little Brown Cow was charging to butt them again, but the witch and the toad flew so fast they undoubtedly are now somewhere beyond the moon.

The fireflies blinked their lights on and off. Cheerful Cat purred happily as the princess held him. The prince, the king, the queen, the knights-in-armor, the duck, the hen, and, of course, Little Brown Cow danced happily around them.

Together they had defeated Mean Old Witch. Together they could share this happiness.

The fireflies lighted the way back to the castle.

The prince asked the princess to marry him.

Little Brown Cow was given her own little field inside the castle walls.

The duck and the hen lived near
Little Brown Cow.

Cheerful Cat visited among all the
people and the animals.

It was a happy castle once more.
Mean Old Witch and Warty Toad were
never seen again.

"ONE DARK NIGHT"

"We All Did It Together..."

4

When the play ended, Miss Clancy stepped out on the stage in front of the curtain and said,

"Thank you for coming to our play. Now we would like to have you meet the author—the little girl who wrote the story 'One Dark Night.' Susy, will you come out here?"

Susy had not taken off her costume. That is how it happened that when she stepped out beside Miss Clancy, everybody stood up and cheered the little brown cow.

Susy smiled. For a moment she could not say a word. She looked over at the side of the stage, and there stood all the boys and girls in their costumes. Then Susy knew what to say:

"We all did it together—the whole second grade class."

Everybody clapped. The mothers, and the fathers, and the brothers, and the sisters, and the grandparents, and the aunts, the teachers, and all the children.

Everybody.

The End